It's time for
COWS IN ACTION!

Genius cow Professor McMoo and
his trusty sidekicks, Pat and Bo,
are star agents of the C.I.A.
– short for COWS IN ACTION!
They travel through time, fighting
evil bulls from the future and
keeping history on the right track . . .

Find out more at
www.cowsinaction.com

Read all the adventures of
McMoo, Pat and Bo:
THE TER-MOO-NATORS
THE MOO-MY'S CURSE
THE ROMAN MOO-STERY
THE WILD WEST MOO-NSTER
THE BATTLE FOR CHRISTMOOS
Coming soon!
THE MOO-GIC OF MERLIN

www.cowsinaction.com

Also by Steve Cole:

ASTROSAURS
Riddle of the Raptors
The Hatching Horror
The Seas of Doom
The Mind-Swap Menace
The Skies of Fear
The Space Ghosts
Day of the Dino-Droids
The Terror-Bird Trap
The Planet of Peril
The Star Pirates
The Claws of Christmas
The Sun-Snatchers
Revenge of the FANG
The Carnivore Curse

Coming soon!
The Dreams of Dread

ASTROSAURS ACADEMY
DESTINATION: DANGER!
CONTEST CARNAGE!
TERROR UNDERGROUND!
JUNGLE HORROR!
Coming soon!
DEADLY DRAMA!

www.astrosaurs.co.uk

THE PIRATE MOO-tiny

Steve Cole

Illustrated by Woody Fox

RED FOX

THE PIRATE MOO-TINY
A RED FOX BOOK 978 1 862 30541 0

First published in Great Britain by Red Fox,
an imprint of Random House Children's Books
A Random House Group Company

This edition published 2009

1 3 5 7 9 10 8 6 4 2

Text copyright © Steve Cole, 2009
Illustrations copyright © Woody Fox, 2009

The Random House Group Limited supports the Forest Stewardship
Council (FSC), the leading international forest certification organization.
All our titles that are printed on Greenpeace-approved FSC-certified paper
carry the FSC logo. Our paper procurement policy can be found at www.
rbooks.co.uk/environment.

Set in Bembo

Red Fox Books are published by Random House Children's Books,
61–63 Uxbridge Road, London W5 5SA

www.**kids**at**random**house.co.uk
www.**rbooks**.co.uk

Addresses for companies within The Random House Group Limited can be
found at: www.randomhouse.co.uk/offices.htm

THE RANDOM HOUSE GROUP Limited Reg. No. 954009

A CIP catalogue record for this book is available from the British Library.

Printed in the UK by CPI Bookmarque, Croydon, CR0 4TD

To Charlie Leonard

★ THE C.I.A. FILES ★

Cows from the present —
Fighting in the past to protect the future . . .

In the year 2550, after thousands of years of being eaten and milked, cows finally live as equals with humans in their own country of Luckyburger. But a group of evil war-loving bulls — the Fed-up Bull Institute — is not satisfied.

Using time machines and deadly ter-moo-nator agents, the F.B.I. is trying to change Earth's history. These bulls plan to enslave all humans and put savage cows in charge of the planet. Their actions threaten to plunge all cowkind into cruel and cowardly chaos . . .

The C.I.A. was set up to stop them.

However, the best agents come not from 2550 — but from the present. From a time in the early 21st century, when the first clever cows began to appear. A time when a brainy bull named Angus McMoo invented the first time machine, little realizing he would soon become the F.B.I.'s number one enemy . . .

COWS OF COURAGE —
TOP SECRET FILES

PROFESSOR ANGUS MCMOO

Security rating: Bravo Moo Zero

Stand-out features: Large white squares on coat, outstanding horns

Character: Scatterbrained, inventive, plucky and keen

Likes: Hot tea, history books, gadgets

Hates: Injustice, suffering, poor-quality tea bags

Ambition: To invent the electric sundial

LITTLE BO VINE

Security rating: For your cow pies only

Stand-out features: Luminous udder (colour varies)

Character: Tough, cheeky, ready-for-anything rebel

Likes: Fashion, chewing gum, self-defence classes

Hates: Bessie Barmer; the farmer's wife

Ambition: To run her own martial arts club for farmyard animals

PAT VINE

Security rating: Licence to fill (stomach with grass)

Stand-out features: Zigzags on coat

Character: Brave, loyal and practical

Likes: Solving problems, anything Professor McMoo does

Hates: Flies not easily swished by his tail

Ambition: To find a five-leaf clover — and to survive his dangerous missions!

Prof. McMoo's
TIMELINE OF NOTABLE
HISTORICAL EVENTS

4.6 billion years BC

PLANET EARTH FORMS

(good job too)

13.7 billion years BC

BIG BANG - UNIVERSE BEGINS

(and first tea atoms created)

23 million years BC

FIRST COWS APPEAR

(23 million is my lucky number!)

1700 BC

SHEN NUNG MAKES FIRST CUP OF TEA

(what a hero!)

7000 BC

FIRST CATTLE KEPT ON FARMS

(Not a great year for cows)

1901 AD

QUEEN VICTORIA DIES

(she was not a-moo-sed)

(by an Egyptian geezer)

2550 BC

GREAT PYRAMID BUILT AT GIZA

31 BC
ROMAN EMPIRE FOUNDED

(Roam-Moo empire founded by a cow but no one remembers that)

1509 AD
HENRY VIII COMES TO THE THRONE

(and probably squashes it)

1066 AD
BATTLE OF HASTINGS

(but what about the Cattle of Hastings?)

1620 AD
ENGLISH PILGRIMS SETTLE IN AMERICA

(bringing with them the first cows to moo in an American accent)

1939 AD
WORLD WAR TWO BEGINS

(or World War Moo as it is known to cows)

2007 AD
I INVENT A TIME MACHINE!!!

2500 AD
COW NATION OF LUCKYBURGER FOUNDED

(HOORAY!)

(about time!)

2550 AD
COWS IN ACTION RECRUIT PROFESSOR McMOO, PAT AND BO

(and now the fun REALLY starts...)

1903 AD
FIRST TEABAGS INVENTED

THE PIRATE MOO-TINY

Chapter One

PIRATES OF THE *COW*-RIBBEAN

Little Bo Vine burst into the cow shed.
"It's holiday time!" she cheered.

Pat Vine jumped so high he nearly hit the rafters. He stared at his big sister in alarm. She was a red-and-white milk cow, who lived as he did on Farmer Barmer's organic farm. But unlike any other cow in the world, she was wearing a pink sparkly swimming

3

costume, strappy sandals and outrageous star-shaped sunglasses.

"Get changed!" he hissed at her. "If anyone sees you in that lot they'll know you're—"

"Funky and cool?" Bo struck a pose.

"They'll know you're not an ordinary cow," said Pat patiently, closing the doors of the shed. "The professor won't like it."

She took off the sunglasses and looked about. "Where is he, anyway?"

"I don't know," Pat admitted. "I've been waiting for him to come back. Perhaps he's off inventing something . . ." He smiled at the thought of Professor

Angus McMoo – brilliant inventor, reckless adventurer, and chairman of the National Farmyards Extreme Tea-Drinking Society (membership: one). While Pat and Bo were certainly clever cattle, Professor McMoo was an out-and-*cow*t genius and truly one of a kind.

How many other bulls were experts on all eras of history?

How many other bulls could tell the difference between 196 different blends of tea?

And how many other bulls would be able to turn their cow shed into a secret, super-amazing TIME MACHINE . . . using only a rusty screwdriver and bits of techno-junk rescued from a scientist's bin?

"Oh, well. I only came in here to see if he had any suntan lotion." Bo threw open the door again. "See you later."

"I told you," said Pat, "you can't walk around like that!"

"I can wear what I want," Bo informed him. "Bessie Barmer's going on holiday today!"

Pat pricked up his ears. "*She is?*" Bessie, the farmer's wife, was a revolting old ratbag with the charm of a pig, the breath of a skunk and the pants of an overweight orang-utan. "For how long?"

charm of a PIG

Breath of a SKUNK

Pants of an overweight orang-utan

"Two whole weeks!" Bo beamed. "She's visiting her cousin in the Caribbean while Farmer Barmer stays here." She pointed with her hoof to the farmhouse. "Look now . . ."

"Right, I'm off!" Bessie yelled at her husband over a stack of suitcases. "Don't be nice to the animals, and get that fence painted before I'm home or there'll be TROUBLE." Pat watched the enormous woman wobble off to a waiting minibus. It lurched and creaked as she clambered on board with her luggage, then it slowly trundled away.

"Yahoooo-*mooooooo*!" cried Bo, doing a funky little dance for joy.

Pat joined in, glad to see the back of the big-bellied bossy boots. Bessie hated the animals and longed to cook them all in a gigantic pie. In fact, it was her rotten nature that had inspired Professor McMoo to build his time machine in the first place — so that he, Pat and Bo could escape the farm for ever.

But things hadn't quite worked out that way. Not once the C.I.A. – the time-travelling, crime-tackling Cows in Action from the twenty-sixth century – had got involved . . .

Pat was jolted from his memories by a high-pitched bleeping sound from up in the cow-shed rafters. He gasped. "Sounds like the secret C.I.A. hotline!"

"That's because it is!" said a muffled voice from nowhere.

Bo jumped into a fighting stance. "Who said that?"

Pat frowned. "The voice seemed to come from under-ground . . ."

"That's because it did!" came the voice again (from

underground). "Hang on a moo . . ."
With a slurping sound, an old, wooden
cupboard slid up from the mud at the
far end of the shed and a large bull
burst out from inside, clutching a mug
of tea. His coat was reddy-brown and
dotted with white
squares. He wore
a pair of chunky
specs on his
nose and a long
curly blonde
wig on his head
– though he
quickly snatched
that off.

"Professor
McMoo!" Pat cried with relief.

"You gave us a fright, Prof," Bo called
over the noisy alarm. "And I almost
gave *you* a kung-*moo* chop!"

"Sorry, but I've just been inventing an
Auto-Dresser machine for our costume

9

store," said McMoo excitedly. "I thought I'd better install it out of sight in the basement, in case Bessie barged in. And it's fantastic – I'm so clever!" He downed his tea in a single gulp. "It will automatically dress us in the perfect outfits for any mission, at any time in history – imagine that!"

"Um, speaking of missions . . ." Pat pointed up into the rafters. "Don't you think you should answer the C.I.A. hotline?"

"Good idea." McMoo tossed the mug over his shoulder and kicked away a hay bale to reveal a large bronze lever in the wall. "That beeping sounds like a strawberry-milkshake alert."

Bo frowned. "You what?"

"It's like a red alert, only thicker and higher in calories – it means there's trouble a-hoof!" McMoo tugged on the lever and the shed started to rattle and shake. The bare wooden walls flipped round to reveal panels packed with high-tech gadgets. A large horseshoe-shaped bank of controls rose up from the secret basement, fed with power from pulsing, multicoloured wires. As a huge computer screen swung down from  the rafters, the transformation was complete: an ordinary cow shed had become an incredible Time Shed, ready to transport its passengers to anywhere in the world, in any time – past, present or future.

The bleeping stopped and the image of a black, burly bull with curly horns appeared, slurping the last drops of his strawberry milkshake. It was Yak, the

rough, tough Director of the C.I.A. "You took your time, Professor," he complained. "I almost had to switch to a *raspberry*-milkshake alert."

"What?!" McMoo gasped. "But . . . that would be terrible!"

"Why, Professor?" asked Pat, wide-eyed.

McMoo shrugged. "Yak doesn't like raspberries."

Bo *blew* a raspberry.

"Yak doesn't like the Fed-up Bull Institute mucking up history, either," said the director sourly. "But that's what the F.B.I. are doing yet again. We've detected a ter-moo-nator on the loose in the year 1718 . . ."

Pat's tummy twisted at the mere mention of ter-moo-nators – deadly, semi-mechanical creatures. The F.B.I. crew were always popping into the past with preposterous plans to take over the world, and these savage robo-bulls were their best agents – fiercely loyal, fiercely efficient and fiercely fierce!

"Whereabouts in 1718?" McMoo wondered.

"Somewhere near Jamaica," Yak told him. "In the Caribbean Sea."

"Pirates!" McMoo shouted. "1718 was a *great* year for pirates of the Caribbean! Blackbeard, Calico Jack Rackham, Black Sam Bellamy . . ."

"What would a ter-moo-nator want with pirates?" Pat wondered.

"Who cares? This is awesome!" cried Bo. "We get to go to the Caribbean almost three hundred years ahead of Bessie Barmer – and I can leave my swimsuit on!"

"You can't," McMoo told her. "Not just because you'd stand out like a

14

cowpat in Buckingham Palace – but because you have to try out my brand-new auto-dresser, remember?"

Bo sighed. "Can't wait."

"This is a serious business, troops," Yak reminded them. "We believe that the F.B.I.'s top inventors have come up with something that could change the world for ever – and not in a good way."

"Don't worry, Yak, we're on the case." McMoo curled his tail around the shed's take-off lever. "Next stop – the *Cow*-ribbean!"

Chapter Two

WORSE THINGS HAPPEN AT SEA

The Time Shed clunked and rattled, crossing oceans of time on course for the Caribbean in 1718.

"What if we land in the water?" Pat fretted. "We might drown!"

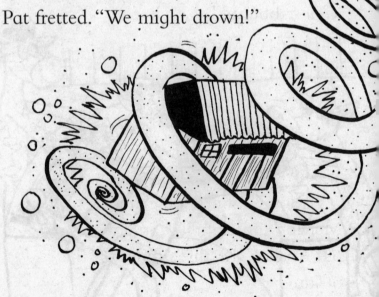

"I've programmed the Time Shed to lock onto any technology that doesn't belong in this era," McMoo assured him. "We should land somewhere close to the F.B.I. base."

"And what if it's an underwater base?" Bo asked.

McMoo considered. "We'll just have to hold our breath!"

The next moment there was a loud, splintering CRUNCH as the Time Shed landed.

Pat gasped. "What was that?"

"A loud, splintering crunch," said McMoo unhelpfully. "Still, we're here! 6th April, 1718, three miles off the coast of Jamaica."

Bo felt the floor rock beneath her hooves. "Hey, what's doing that?"

McMoo carefully opened the doors. A salty, rotten stench rolled in from the darkness outside, and the cattle gazed out on a shadowy landscape of large wooden crates. "Of course!" cried the professor. "We've landed *inside* a sailing ship! Not on top of it in full view of the crew . . . not underneath it, frightening the fish . . . but *inside* it! Imagine that. Such steering! Such timing!"

"Such a fluke," said Bo dryly. "Whereabouts inside the ship are we?"

The professor gave her a slightly huffy look. "In the hold – where the sailors keep their cargo and everything they need for the journey."

Pat grimaced. "So that crunch we heard was the shed squashing their supplies?"

"Afraid so!" Then McMoo heard a noise, and the faint glow of a distant oil

lamp lit the shadows. "Shh!" he hissed, shutting the doors. "Someone's coming!"

"That was a terrible noise, right enough," came a rough voice. "I thought Blackbeard himself was firing cannons at us!"

"Well, we're not taking in water," said another. "Probably just rotten timbers falling. Anyway, Blackbeard wouldn't bother with us — not with *our* cargo. Come on, let's get aloft."

The glow of the lamp disappeared.

"Phew!" Pat whispered. "Those sailors didn't spot the shed in the gloom."

"There are loads of old crates down here," said Bo, "who'd notice another one?" Then she saw McMoo glower at her and quickly changed the subject. "So who was this Blackbeard bloke, then? Some rubbishy old pirate?"

"The man's a legend!" McMoo turned to the screen hanging from the Time-

Shed rafters. "Computer, give us the Blackbeard file."

Blackbeard. ++Notorious pirate. ++Real name Edward Teach. ++Born approx 1689. ++Went to sea at an early age. ++Grew a very big and scary beard. ++Guess what — it was black! ++Teach and his beard turned to piracy in 1713, robbing ships, spreading terror and being generally nasty. ++The rascal even marooned twenty-five of his own pirates before they could start a mutiny against him.

"What's a moo-tiny?" asked Bo. "A very small moo?"

"*Mutiny*," McMoo corrected her.

"It's when sailors turn against those in charge and take control of the ship themselves."

"Cool!" said Bo. "And what's 'moo-rooned'?"

"*Maroon*ing someone is a classic pirate punishment – it means dumping them on a desert island with no way of getting off. But never mind all that . . ." McMoo ran over to the big wardrobe on the other side of the shed. "Let's try out my auto-dresser. You up for it, Pat?"

"Yes, please!" Pat trotted over and stood in the cupboard doorway.

"I've set the controls for spring, 1718!" McMoo pressed a big red button on the side of the cupboard. "Here we go . . ."

Two spindly metal arms shot out from the cupboard and pulled Pat inside. They tugged a silk stocking over his head, shoved a black boot on one hoof, wrapped his legs in a frilly shirt and stuck a top hat onto his bottom. Then the metal arms bundled him out and folded away again.

"*Mmmmmmpfff!*" Pat cried as he fell over.

"Hmm," said McMoo, switching off the machine. "Not a *total* success . . ."

"But totally funny!" Bo chortled.

"Probably just a dodgy circuit." McMoo removed a slim metal box from inside the cupboard. "I'll fix it later. Meanwhile, we'll have to rummage round as usual!"

By the time Pat had untangled himself, Bo had squeezed into a pale-blue gown with three-quarter-length sleeves and a big hooped skirt. A cloth

23

bonnet covered her head. "This look is lame," she complained. "Can't I rip up the dress a bit and add a pink crocodile-skin coat?"

"No," said McMoo firmly. He looked every inch the wealthy gentleman in his navy waistcoat, breeches and stockings.

Pat found some grey breeches and a white shirt with baggy sleeves. Then he put on his ringblender − a vital bit of C.I.A. kit that looked like a large silver nose ring. Cows who wore them could pass themselves off as human beings; the clever gadgets even allowed cows and humans to understand each other in any age and place. But as Pat passed ringblenders to Bo and the professor, he reminded himself that only humans would be fooled. Any lurking F.B.I. agents would see through the disguise at once − and attack . . .

"Come on then," said McMoo impatiently, jamming a smart white wig and a tricorn hat over his horns to complete his look. "We're on a real eighteenth-century cargo boat! And don't forget, the Time Shed was drawn to technology that doesn't belong in this area – which could mean there's a ter-moo-nator close by." He grinned and charged out of the doors. "Let's explore!"

"I suppose we have to," said Pat nervously, as he and Bo followed McMoo out into the darkness of the hold. It was stiflingly hot, and the air was thick with the tang of salt and tar-painted timbers. Almost straight away, Pat tripped over the remains of a fancy armchair shattered by the shed's arrival. Other bits of damaged expensive furniture lay scattered about.

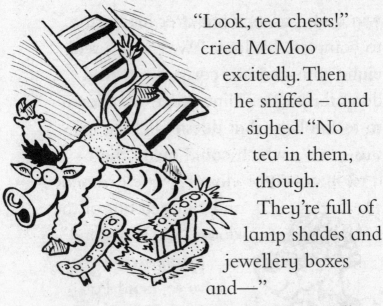

"Look, tea chests!" cried McMoo excitedly. Then he sniffed – and sighed. "No tea in them, though. They're full of lamp shades and jewellery boxes and—"

"*Very* big dresses," Bo reported, pulling out a huge bundle of satin frills from one of the chests. "Funny sort of cargo."

The ship was large, and the cattle had to troop up three flights of narrow wooden stairs before they reached daylight on the main deck. The sun was shining. Huge sails, white against the deep-blue sky, were being tended by busy seamen in the rigging.

Then suddenly, Pat heard clomping footsteps from further along the deck.

26

He ducked back behind the hatch that led directly down to the hold, and McMoo and Bo did the same.

"Your ship is rubbish," moaned a familiar female voice. "It's so slow, and everyone on board is smelly . . ."

"Oh, no!" Pat groaned. "That sounds like—"

"Bessie Barmer," McMoo agreed grimly. "Or rather, one of her ancestors."

Bo peered over the top of the hatch. A tall, bewhiskered man in a square-necked vest and white trousers was walking beside a large Bessie look-alike in a vast black dress.

"Bessie has relatives in the Caribbean," Pat recalled. "Just our luck to run straight into one from 1718!"

"The *Doodle-Doo* has only been at sea for three days," the woman's companion said wearily. "And despite strong winds, we're due to arrive in Jamaica tomorrow. You really must learn to be

27

patient, my dear."

"Don't you 'my dear' me, Captain
Cove!" growled Bessie's double. "I'm
Annie-Beth Barmer – the wealthiest
widow in all Carolina. I'm too rich
to be patient! Now I've bought the
most super-pricey mega-mansion in all
Jamaica, I just want to shift my stuff
there and be done with it."

"So it's Annie-Beth's stuff we squashed
in the hold," Pat realized. "Oops!"

Bo giggled. "Never mind, eh?"

"Why can't we go faster," Annie-
Beth whined on crossly. "Like *that* ship
over there?"

"What ship?" Captain Cove looked

out to sea – and gasped. "Gad, look
at that flag – it's a *pirate* ship!" He
shouted up at the sailors in the rigging.
"Look lively, men! Pirates ahoy, heading
straight for us! We can't outrun them, so
we'll have to fight . . ." Leaving Annie-
Beth flapping and fluttering, the captain
ran off along the deck to warn the rest
of his crew.

"A pirate ship!" McMoo seemed
delighted. "This I have to see!"

Pat and Bo followed the professor as
he crept out of hiding. Sure enough, a
tall ship with a sharp bow was slicing
through the Caribbean waves towards
them. A big, black flag marked with a
skull and crossbones fluttered from the
tallest mast – only this particular skull
had two horns attached.

Then McMoo caught
a flash of silver
from the deck of
the approaching

clipper. Was it a cannon? A crossly waved cutlass, perhaps? With an uneasy feeling, he pulled a pair of mini-binoculars from his pocket and took a closer look . . .

A huge, powerful figure was perched on the prow of the pirate ship. Sharp steel horns stuck out from its head. One green eye glowed beneath the brim of a three-cornered hat; the other was masked by an enormous eye patch. An outrageous black beard hid the rest of its face from view. The figure held strange weapons in both iron hooves.

"Is it that Pink-Eyebrow bloke?" wondered Bo.

"Blackbeard," Pat corrected her.

"I only wish it was." McMoo dropped the binoculars and turned to Pat and Bo. "That's no ordinary pirate captain — it's a ter-moo-nator!"

Chapter Three

THE MENACE OF MOOBEARD

Bo blinked. "A pirate ter-moo-nator?"

"Yes. And he's not wearing a ringblender," McMoo added. "Must be trying to look as scary as possible to intimidate his victims, just like real pirates used to do."

"He's succeeding," said Pat. "I think I need the toilet!"

"Who said that?" Annie-Beth Barmer looked over her shoulder – and gasped to see McMoo and his friends. "*Help!*" she bellowed. "Pirates! Cut-throats!"

Hearing her alarm, Captain Cove came charging back along the deck, his sword drawn at the ready. But at the

sight of the three newcomers, he skidded
to a stop. "Great Scott!"

"Nope, Angus McMoo, actually.
Although I do come from a family
of great Scots, so you were close. . ."
The professor grinned. "Allow me to
introduce my nephew, Patrick Vine and
Bonnie, my niece."

"They're pirates!" Annie-Beth insisted.
"Or nasty, rotten stowaways!"

"Their clothes are too clean to be
either." Cove narrowed his eyes. "I'm
Roger Cove, skipper of the *Doodle-Doo.*

Where did you come from?"

"Those pirates sank our ship just this morning," said Pat quickly. "We escaped in a rowing boat and came aboard your fine craft in search of aid."

"Nice one, bruv," Bo whispered.

"I'm afraid it is you who must aid us," said Cove, looking grimly at the approaching pirate ship. "If you've fought those rascals before, you can help us fight them now."

"We'll 'doodle-doo' all we can to help!" McMoo assured him.

Pat felt his tummy turn as Captain Cove ordered the crew to different positions on deck. The pirates' ship – the *Beefy Bandit* – was gaining on them fast. With a roar like thunder, a cannon fired from its side, tearing a ragged hole in the *Doodle-Doo*'s mainsail. Bo ducked as another orange-sized cannonball smashed splinters of wood from the mizzenmast.

Captain Cove raised his sword and ordered his men to return fire. Soon the air was thick with the bang and flash of pistols. Then, Cove's crew stopped firing.

"Look, Cap'n!" a sailor shouted, pointing in horror to the ter-moo-nator standing proudly at the *Beefy Bandit*'s bow. "What is *that*?"

"'Tis a creature from the darkest pits o' the sea!" wailed another, dropping his gun in fear.

"Or a monster from eight hundred years in the future," Pat muttered.

"I am Moobeard!" the ter-moo-nator roared robotically, waving a huge cutlass as the *Beefy Bandit* pulled up alongside the *Doodle-Doo*. Twenty angry

pirates were gathered behind him. "Yes, Moobeard. Most evil pirate of the high seas – and the low seas too. I make even the terrible Blackbeard himself seem like a beginner!"

Captain Cove gulped. "Perhaps I should surrender."

"And let those pirates take my priceless possessions?" Annie-Beth cried. "Never!" But then Moobeard and his men pulled out enormous, gleaming guns. "Er . . . then again, if they *really* want them . . ."

"Those things look familiar," said Pat.

"Butter-bazookas!" McMoo realized. "Quickly, everyone, hit the deck!"

Everyone dived for cover – except Bo, who took McMoo at his word and whacked the deck hard with her hoof. "Why d'you want me to hit it, anyway?" she asked. "Wouldn't a kick be better?" She slammed down her hoof again – and with a splintering crack, the plank beneath her broke in two! With a startled "*Moooo!*" she dropped out of sight . . .

"Bo!" Pat cried — just as waves of smelly, rancid butter squirted across from the pirate ship. The greasy goo splashed everywhere, and Captain Cove's men were soon dowsed in the stinky stuff, slipping and skidding helplessly over the deck. Cove himself cried out in agony — not because of the butter, but because Annie-Beth fainted and fell on top of him with a THUD.

McMoo and Pat tried to help up the sailors as the disgusting dairy slop rained down about them. But it was hopeless. They skidded about the slimy wood like mad ice skaters.

"Cease fire, me hearties!" Moobeard bellowed in his scary, mechanical voice. "Put on your non-slip shoes, take everyone prisoner and steer their ship back home. I will wait for you there."

"Aye-aye, Moobeard!" the pirates
shouted. They threw out boarding nets
to cover the gap between the two vessels
and started to swarm across.

"Hey!" Bo's voice floated up from
out of the hole in the deck. "What's
happening? I think I just squashed some
more furniture . . ."

"Bo!" Pat cried with relief. "You're
OK!"

"Shhh, Pat." As the pirates scrambled
on board, McMoo slithered over to the
hole. "Bo, listen!" he hissed. "The pirates

have caught us. Stay out of sight – we'll need you to rescue us later."

"Shall I take out my ringblender, so they'll think I'm just a cow?"

"No, don't!" McMoo urged her. "Pirates spend most of their lives at sea, living on rum, rock-hard biscuits and the occasional turtle – they'll roast you as soon as look at you!"

"OK, I'll hide in the Time Shed," Bo grumbled. "Be careful."

"You too," Pat added. And just as the pirates stomped and splashed over the sludgy, yellow deck, he shifted his bottom to hide the hole from view.

"Nobody move," snarled an ugly, warty pirate with long, greasy hair. "I'm Gaptooth. Do as I says, or I'll cut

off yer toes and feed 'em to the seagulls!"

"Kindly remember there are ladies present!" said Cove.

"Er, '*Lady* present,' you mean," said McMoo quickly. He winked at Cove so that the captain knew to keep quiet about Bo. "There are no other women on board."

"Is that a woman?" Gaptooth peered down at the sleeping Annie-Beth, doubtfully. "Well, lads, we'd best search the ship for other passengers and loot – and then set sail for Udderdoom Island!"

The other pirates clapped and cheered as they fanned out across the deck.

"It's strange," McMoo murmured to Pat. "Why does that ter-moo-nator want to steer this ship back to his buccaneering base? Any ordinary pirate would just take his treasure and push off again . . ."

"Stop yer yabbering!" growled

Gaptooth. "We'll teach ye scurvy knaves what it means to be prisoners of the most diabolical demon ever to loot the high seas . . . and it be a lesson you won't soon forget!"

In the Time Shed, Bo hid up in the rafters, chewing on her gum tensely. She could hear pirates poking about in the hold outside. Soon, they started to rattle the shed's doors.

"It's locked fast!" one pirate growled. "Leave it till we reach Udderdoom Island," another said. "Moobeard is strong as an iron walrus. He'll open it with his little finger."

"A-harr," the first pirate agreed. "But there could be someone hiding inside. I've got a taper here, treated with sulphur

– let's light it and smoke the lubber out . . ."

Bo frowned as the lit taper – a burning strip of waxed paper – was shoved under the shed doors. Within moments, it was belching poisonous smoke. She could put out the taper, of course. But then the pirates would know she was inside, break down the doors and catch her – how would she ever rescue Pat and the professor? Yet, if she stayed inside she would choke, and the pirates would hear that too . . .

What am I going to do? Bo thought helplessly, holding her breath as the evil fumes grew thicker around her. *What?*

Chapter Four

THE ISLAND OF FEAR

Bo could feel herself growing dizzy. The
dense, stinking smoke was all around,
and the breath she was holding wouldn't
last for ever…

*But it could last a bit longer with a little
help!* Bo realized. Holding her nose
to keep out the fumes, she chewed
her gum, pressed it
against her teeth
and then carefully
blew out. Her breath
inflated an enormous
bubble-gum bubble!
With equal care,
she recycled the air

by breathing in again. The huge, pink bubble shrivelled as she did this, so she breathed out once more to re-inflate it.

A couple of minutes went by. Bo's single breath of air, trapped inside the bubble gum, was getting decidedly stale. Her lungs were bursting, her head was spinning more and more but she kept tight hold of the rafters . . .

And then, finally, the smoke began to thin out. "There's no one in there," the first pirate decided. "Let's search elsewhere."

"You do that," gasped Bo, spitting out her well-chomped gum and dropping down from the rafters in a heap. Panting for breath and trying not to choke, she lay down to get her strength back.

Something told Bo she was going to need it . . .

Warm darkness was starting to fall over the Caribbean. Tied-up on deck with Cove and his crew – and the still sleeping Annie-Beth Barmer – Pat felt a pang of fear as the craggy cliffs of Udderdoom Island came into sight. Two gigantic mountains curved up to the purple sky like giant bull horns, and a staggeringly large and scary bull-face had been carved into the rock. The island shores were wreathed in an eerie mist. It seemed a grim, forbidding place.

Professor McMoo gave Pat a comforting smile. "Not the perfect Caribbean getaway, is it?"

"At least the pirates haven't found Bo," Pat muttered.

"Shut yer traps," snarled Gaptooth.

Pat soon realized it was good advice, as the strange mist came swirling out to engulf the *Doodle-Doo*. It tasted acrid and smelled horrible. Everyone began to cough and choke, even Gaptooth and his grizzled band.

"That's not real mist," Pat spluttered.

"No, it's some kind of chemical fog," the professor agreed. "It's harder to see through than normal mist. Perhaps it's here to hide Moobeard's home from prying eyes."

After a minute or so, the smoke cleared a little. Pat gulped as he saw more sailing ships looming silently over them on either side. There were all kinds of boats, anchored in a large harbour.

"Quite a collection," McMoo observed.

"I count twenty ships," said Cove gravely. "With a fleet like that, Moobeard can raid anywhere. Even the fearsome Blackbeard has only four vessels."

McMoo nodded. "But the question is . . . what does Moobeard do with the ships' passengers and crew?"

Gaptooth gave a low, sinister chuckle as the shadowy cliffs of Udderdoom Island closed in around them.

Bo jumped up from the floor of the shed at the sound of far-off shouting.

"Heave to!" a hoarse voice yelled, and Bo felt the ship starting to slow.

"Drop anchor!" came another voice.

We've arrived, thought Bo. She was itching to charge out, set free Pat and the professor and fight the pirates to a standstill. But she knew she'd have

a better chance if she could sneak in
undetected.

After a tense hour had inched past, Bo
crept back up to the slimy, slippery deck
and the gathering gloom of the tropical
night. The *Doodle-Doo* was as quiet as
a watery grave. "The pirates must have
taken everyone ashore by now," she
reasoned. "And I bet they'll want to
celebrate before they come back and
divvy up the loot. I know *I* would!"

Bo gazed out over the deserted ships and barren landscape of the island before her. There was a large wooden door set into the nearest cliff, with a half-dozen pirate guards keeping watch outside. Even if she got past them, opening that door would be another matter.

"Perhaps there's a back way," she said to herself.

Bo stripped down to the swimsuit she still wore beneath her dress, stuffed her hat and dress down the front of it, and then dived into the warm sea. She swam for the wooden jetty built onto the rocky shore. The smoky darkness helped to hide her

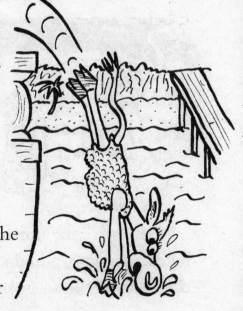

as she clambered up the steep cliff, more like a mountain goat than a cow.

Finally, panting for breath, she reached the summit of the slope – and stared in amazement.

Ahead of her was a wide-open meadow filled with the lushest, most munchable grass that Bo had ever seen. Overcome with sudden hunger, she tore into the greenery. Her tongue fizzed with the flavour and she ate more and more until her stomach was full.

"Dee-lish," she murmured. With a belch, she got up and skirted round the edge of the succulent meadow, still looking for another way into Moobeard's lair. She ducked down again as she spotted some more pirates, carefully digging up the tasty turf with shovels and piling up the pieces in a wheelbarrow. "What are they up to?" she wondered.

"*MOOOO!*" Bo jumped at the sound of a bull. It was coming from a wooden shack standing on the meadow just a few hundred metres away. Could Pat or the Professor be inside? Or was it a fed-up bull from the F.B.I.? Another, deeper "*moooooooo*" came from the shack, so Bo scurried over to investigate.

Peeping through a crack in the wooden wall, Bo saw a grey bull and a black-and-white milk cow standing sullenly inside with thick metal collars about their necks, each chained to a concrete post.

"Prisoners," she breathed. "Probably all set to become a pirate's tea!"

Checking that the men with shovels were looking the other way, Bo sneaked inside. "Your troubles are over, buddies!" Bo beamed at the cattle. "Your very own cow superhero is here to get you out!"

But as soon as he saw her, the grey bull lunged forwards and butted Bo in the stomach!

"*Oof!*" Bo gasped. Luckily the dress she had packed down the front of her swimming costume absorbed some of the blow's force. "What did you do that for?"

"*Moooooo!*" The milk cow reared up on her back legs, jabbing out with her hooves and bopping Bo on the udder.

"Ow! That does it!" Bo growled. "If you two want a scrap, you can have one!" She raised her hooves – then felt dizzy. "Hang on," she said. "We're all cattle. We're on the same side. Why *should* we fight?"

The bull responded with a savage "*MOOOOO!*" Eyes bulging, horns like giant ivory daggers, he heaved desperately against his collar.

"No, bull. You're doing it all wrong."
Bo sighed. "Look, if you exert a large
tensile force on the chain itself, it will
break at the weakest link . . ." Suddenly,
she shook her head. "What's wrong with
me? I sound like the professor!"

But taking her advice, the bull
stamped on its chain, raised his neck
and broke free! He butted Bo in the
belly again and she fell down on the
grass. The milk cow sniggered and used
the same chain-breaking strategy as the
bull. In only a few seconds she'd broken
free too.

"I don't want to fight," Bo told them.
"Needless violence is so distasteful."
Then she frowned. "Hang on – I *always*
want to fight! What's wrong with me?"

Dazed and confused, Bo barely
noticed the mad bull and the cow as
they charged towards her . . .

Chapter Five

AT THE MERCY OF MOOBEARD

An angry *moo* from the grey bull alerted
Bo to danger. She saw that he would
reach her before the milk cow did – so
she whipped out her bonnet and threw
it over his head, covering his eyes
completely! The bull tried to shake off
the hat, butting the charging cow as he
did so. Deflected from her course, she
missed Bo by millimetres and crashed
straight through the wall of the shack,
while the bull rolled around on the
ground in blind panic.

Bo snatched back her hat and fled
outside, jumping into some nearby
bushes. "What's their problem?" she

wondered. "I only wanted to set them free." Then she saw the turf-digging pirates come running.

"Them cows have gone proper wild this time!" the biggest pirate said. He pulled a shiny gun from a holster around his waist – Bo recognized it as a sour-cream squirter. 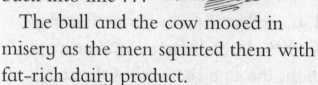 "Well, a few sprays of this will bring them back into line . . ."

The bull and the cow mooed in misery as the men squirted them with fat-rich dairy product.

Bo sighed. "No good crying over spilled sour cream. I've got to find Pat and the professor." She swayed dizzily. "If only I didn't feel so strange . . ."

Silent as a mouse – albeit a large,

dazed red-and-brown mouse with
an udder — Bo crept away through
the moonlit cliff tops in search of her
friends.

Hundreds of metres beneath Bo's hooves
and quite unaware of her predicament,
Professor McMoo and Pat sat in a
small stone cell. They had been locked
up together with Annie-Beth and the
twelve-strong crew of the *Doodle-Doo*.
    "When's your idiot niece going to
rescue us, Professor?" wailed Annie-Beth.
"Those evil pirates will kill us all!"

McMoo shook his head. "If they wanted to kill us, why not do it straight away?"

But Annie-Beth would not be reassured. "Then ... they must want to make me their pirate queen!"

"They're not that stupid," said Pat, and the other men nodded in agreement.

Suddenly, a key rattled in the cell door and a gaggle of sword-wielding pirates pressed in. Their leader was a dirty, stinky old man with a steel hook where his right hand had once been. "Come with us, lubbers."

"Who are you?" Cove demanded.

The man passed wind. "Men call me
... Long-Pong Silver!"

"I can't think why," gasped McMoo.

"Shift, ye lily-livered dogs!" Long-
Pong smiled nastily. "Moobeard wants
to see ye, and he don't like to be kept
waiting. His temper makes the rage of
Blackbeard himself seem like that of a
mildly irritated hamster!"

Pat gasped, the sailors exchanged
nervous looks and Annie-Beth groaned
with fear. But McMoo just beamed.
"This is lovely! I wanted to have a chat.
Perhaps even a cuppa ..."

Long-Pong and
his friends herded
McMoo and the
others through dark,
dead-straight tunnels,
eventually taking a
passage that ended at
a large, bronze door.

The *Doodle-Doo*ers were shoved into
a rectangular rocky chamber, lit with
bright torches and decorated with
sumptuous tapestries. To Pat's surprise,
crowds of people were standing around
inside. There had to be two hundred or
more, some talking in nervous huddles,
some slouching in silence.

"Gad!" cried Captain Cove. "I know
some of these men. That's a French
merchant based in nearby Tortuga . . .
Yonder Spaniard commands a clipper
from Hispaniola . . ."

"Oh! And that Dutchman over there
was a friend of my late husband!"
Annie-Beth pointed at a large man,
then smiled coyly. "He rather liked me
as I recall. The cheeky devil!"

The Dutchman looked at her with
horror, and hurried away.

"Professor," said Pat, "these people
must have arrived on those ships outside."

"Passengers and crew from all over

Europe, captured with their cargoes off the coasts of the New World," McMoo agreed thoughtfully. "Whatever does Moobeard want with them all?"

Pat clutched the professor's arm. "I think we're about to find out!"

The room fell silent. All eyes turned to one end of the chamber, where Moobeard marched onto a low stage. Pat felt his legs quiver at the sheer size of the ter-moo-nator – and the length of his beard, which hung down over his metal face like two overweight squirrels. The pirate chief's one green eye scanned the room emotionlessly.

"Don't let him spot you," McMoo warned Pat quietly. "He'll see through our ringblenders and know the C.I.A. sent us."

Pat nodded and ducked behind Annie-Beth Barmer. Since there was plenty of room for two, the professor joined him.

"Greetings, helpless prisoners," said Moobeard in his low, grating voice. "You are completely in my power."

"Don't kill me!" Annie-Beth beseeched him. "Kill everyone else if you like, but please, not me! I'll give you all my money! I'll give you everything I own! I'll give you *kisses*!"

"I'll give you to the sharks if you don't shut up!" Moobeard retorted.

"They'd probably give her back," Pat muttered.

"And now I have gathered you all here . . ." The ter-moo-nator gave an evil smile. "I shall send you back to your ships and let you go."

For a few seconds there was shocked silence. Then a ragged cheer went up from some of the relieved prisoners.

"But why would you do such a

thing?" asked the French merchant suspiciously.

"So you will go back to your homelands and spread the terror of my name!" Moobeard nodded. "Tell your leaders of my fearful appearance. Tell them that I am better than boring Blackbeard could ever be. And warn them that I will *never* show mercy again." He turned and headed towards a door at the back of the stage. "Have a safe trip. Goodbye!"

Professor McMoo looked worried. "That tin-pot pirate is up to something. If he lets these people go, he'll have the naval fleets of half-a-dozen countries on his doorstep within the week."

Pat nodded. "He must know he can't fight them all. Perhaps he's planning to abandon this base?"

"Ye'll never know, lubber!" A terrible smell assaulted Pat's nostrils and he turned to find Long-Pong towering over him. "Ye and yer friend here b'aint going nowhere! Moobeard spied ye as ye came aboard, and it seems he has other plans for ye . . ."

"A nice cup of tea, perhaps?" McMoo suggested.

Pat gulped. "Professor, I think we've been rumbled!"

Cove scowled at the pirates. "Don't you dare hurt them."

"At least, not till I've gone," Annie-Beth added. "I faint at the sight of blood!"

"So do I," McMoo assured her. "And in any case, I'm afraid Pat and I have

other plans – Plan A, for instance . . ."

The professor shoved Long-Pong aside and bundled Pat towards the exit. But it was no good. The way out was clogged with anxious sailors and merchantmen desperate to leave. And more pirates, led by Gaptooth, were coming for the two C.I.A. agents with swords drawn.

"So much for Plan A," cried Pat. "What's Plan B?"

"Pretty similar to Plan A, actually," said McMoo. "Only this time we run a bit faster!" He charged towards the stage. "Moobeard left through the back door, perhaps we can do the same . . ."

But as they neared the door, it swung open to reveal Moobeard himself staring balefully down at them.

". . . or perhaps not," McMoo concluded. He and Pat turned to run again. But Gaptooth, Long-Pong and the other pirates were already closing in.

"Er . . . Plan C?" asked Pat.

With a triumphant roar, Moobeard grabbed McMoo and Pat by the scruffs of their necks. "Plan C, C.I.A. scum," he grated, "is that you shall both *DIE!*"

Chapter Six

DOOMED FOR SHORE!

Moobeard himself frogmarched Pat and
McMoo out of the rocky chamber, back
down the dank, sinister tunnels and into
an empty cell.

The C.I.A. agents were left waiting
for hours with no food or water.

Then suddenly, Moobeard reappeared
with Gaptooth, Long-Pong and another
pirate, as big as the other two put
together. Pat and the professor were
taken out to a moonlit beach beside
the harbour. The craggy cliffs loomed
behind them like black shadows against
the star-splashed sky. The mysterious
mist swirled eerily over the sea like a

huge ghost caressing the water.

Pat's pounding heart skipped a beat as he made out two huge holes in the white sand ahead of him, close to the lapping sea. Almost casually, the ter-moo-nator dropped Pat into one hole and McMoo into another.

"You will *not* inform the C.I.A. of my activities here." The robo-pirate turned to Gaptooth. "Bury them up to their necks."

Gaptooth sniggered. "Aye-aye, cap'n. Ahoy, there, Big Pete – give me a hand."

The giant pirate grunted, stepped forward and grabbed a shovel.

"You can't do this!" Pat shouted, as a spadeful of sand showered over him. "When the tide comes in, the waters will rise up over our heads. We'll drown!"

"Correct," said Moobeard. "You shall perish here, all alone."

"Why have you let your other prisoners go?" demanded McMoo. "Just what are you up to?"

Long-Pong cleared his throat. ". . . I was wondering that myself, Cap'n," he said. "'Tis madness to let good prisoners go without setting a ransom."

Moobeard grabbed Long-Pong by the throat. "You question my decisions?" His silver face turned angry red and his enormous beard began to smoke. "Cross me again and I shall macaroon you!"

"That's *maroon*, not macaroon!" said McMoo. "Unless you meant you were going to pelt him with coconut-flavoured cookies?"

"Be silent!" The ter-moo-nator hurled Long-Pong into the sea, where he landed with a colossal *splash*. "No one may question a ter-moo-nator!"

Gaptooth frowned. "No one may question a what?"

"Sometimes he doesn't act like a real pirate at all, does he, Gaptooth?" the professor said quietly. "He's not like Blackbeard, is he?"

"I am better than Blackbeard!" grumbled the robo-bull. "Now, be silent or . . . or I shall splice your giblets from bellybutton to shoulder. Ha-harrrrrr!"

"Oh, very convincing," McMoo jeered. "Why do you even bother to follow him, Gaptooth?"

"He has mighty powers," Gaptooth growled.

"And he brings in loot," said Big Pete.

"And besides, Blackbeard's got no vacancies at the moment," Long-Pong muttered, wading back out of the sea. With a nervous look at Moobeard, he picked up a spade and joined in the work as best he could. Soon, Pat and McMoo stood buried upright, with only their heads poking out of the sand.

"Now, Gaptooth," droned Moobeard. "Inspect the engines. Make sure they are ready to operate before the navy can come after us."

"Engines?" McMoo frowned. "*Siege* engines, you mean – giant catapults and battering rams?"

"You will never know." Moobeard stared down gloatingly at his captives. "Farewell, C.I.A. fools. I go to inform F.B.I. High Command of my success. Long-Pong, Big Pete – guard them."

71

"Arrrrrr," said Big Pete, as Moobeard and Gaptooth stalked away. He pulled a butter-bazooka from his great leather belt. Long-Pong pulled out a sour-cream squirter and sat down on a rock to wait.

Long, scary minutes passed by. The hissing sea crept slowly closer like a vast, hungry animal. First it lapped against Pat's neck. Then it splashed his chin. McMoo flinched as a wave broke over his face. He gasped, rocking slightly from side to side, a look of great concentration on his face.

Pat sighed. "If only Bo were here to save us!"

"If only *I* had a change of outfit," said McMoo, his eyes agleam. "Hmm. Hang on a minute. If my one-hoofed alterations have only worked . . ."

Suddenly, the water in front of McMoo began to churn and bubble. Small lumps of wet sand burst out from around his head and flew through the air. Pat stared in amazement, while Big Pete and Long-Pong jumped up in alarm.

Then two spindly metal hands broke the surface of the water, flicking the sand this way and that. "Hey!" Pat grinned in amazement. "That's the auto-dresser from the costume cupboard!"

"Right!" McMoo beamed as he hauled himself out of the churned-up sand. "As it turns out, rubbish for changing clothes, but great for tunnelling through wet sand! I slipped it in my pocket so I could fix it later — but it works well enough to get us *out* of a fix!"

Pat gasped as Long-Pong and Pete lumbered towards McMoo, weapons raised. "We're not out of it yet!"

McMoo ducked as Long-Pong fired a sour-cream blast. He hurled the auto-dresser at the pirate. Its jerking mechanical hands tugged Long-Pong's shirt up over his head and pulled his trousers down around his ankles so he stumbled and fell.

But then Big Pete grabbed the

whirling arms of the auto-dresser in one fat hand and crushed them into scrap metal. McMoo swung a hoof at Pete – but the burly pirate dodged aside and punched the professor on the conk! He fell with a salty *sploosh* in the water.

Long-Pong scrambled back up with the sour-cream squirter. Pete raised his butter-bazooka. As McMoo struggled to rise, and as Pat heaved helplessly against the heavy sand pressing down upon him, the pirates prepared to open fire . . .

"Wait!" called a familiar female voice. "Don't do it!"

Pat groaned with relief. "Little Bo!"

"Right in the nick of time!" McMoo grinned. "Our milky-clean fighting machine will soon sort out these pesky pirates!"

They watched, waiting for Bo to burst into action. But she didn't. Instead, she smoothed out her skirts and smiled at Big Pete and Long-Pong. "Put down your guns, boys. Violence is never the answer, you know."

"What?" Pat spluttered through a mouthful of sea water. "Bo, is that really you speaking?"

But Bo ignored her brother. "Chill out,

pirates. Give peace a chance! What do you say?"

Big Pete smiled nastily and pointed the butter-bazooka at her. "No!"

Bo frowned. "Now, hold on! I'm standing less than two point six metres away from you. At that distance, there's a ninety-three per cent chance that a butter-blast of as little as one-and-a half seconds' duration could cause me a serious injury . . ."

"Good!" roared Big Pete, as he set the bazooka to maximum power and squeezed the trigger . . .

Chapter Seven

ESCAPE OAR DIE!

Just as red-hot runny butter surged from the nozzle of the gun towards Bo, McMoo dragged Pete's aim downwards with a well-placed hoof. The molten mess soaked the sand behind Pat's head, and fierce heat prickled the young bull's hide.

"That's right . . ." McMoo wrestled with the huge pirate, struggling to hold the weapon in position. "Just a little longer . . ."

Long-Pong couldn't get a clear shot with his squirter so he grabbed McMoo in a neck lock. The pirate's lethal hook edged closer to McMoo's face.

"Help me, Bo!" the professor gasped.

"OK," Bo agreed. "Look, pirates, no hard feelings – let's all sit around a table and discuss our problems ..."

"What's *your* problem, Bo?" Pat demanded. But, as the rancid butter rained down, he could feel his sandy prison squelching and bubbling, giving way ... Finally, straining with all his might, he pulled himself free and kicked Long-Pong's feet from under him. Again, the pirate went down with a splash – this time into the hot butter.

"I don't approve of violence," McMoo gasped, "but this is self-defence!" So saying, he lowered his horns and butted Big Pete into the air.

"Yeooowwww! *UMPHH!*" The pirate landed headfirst in the steaming sand with his legs sticking in the air.

"Cheer up," McMoo told him. "Maybe you'll find buried treasure while you're down there!" Then he turned to Bo. "Now, what's going on? How come you started talking percentages to that pirate instead of punching him?"

"I couldn't believe it!" Pat gave her a sandy hug. "It's great to see you, but you're acting really weird."

"I know. I don't know what's wrong with me." Tears brimmed in Bo's eyes. "That's twice now I haven't wanted to fight! The very thought of a scrap gives me the shakes. *And . . .*" She gulped. "I've gone all brainy!"

"*You?*" Pat spluttered. "Prove it!

Bo folded her arms. "326 x 987 equals 321,762."

McMoo frowned. "Correct!"

Pat was astounded. "Tell me, what's

79

the square root of 24,503?"

Bo yawned. "156.5343412801."

"Close enough!" McMoo stared at her. "Bo, what's happened? You're almost as clever as I am!"

"Wait," said Pat, staring down at the buttery sand. "We're a pirate short. Where's Long-Pong gone?"

"He must have sneaked away," McMoo cried. "He'll raise the alarm for sure."

Pat groaned. "We've got to get out of here!"

"I passed an old rowing boat in the harbour when I sneaked down here. It must have fallen from one of the big ships." Bo stooped to pick up the butter-bazooka and the sour-cream squirter. "Come on!"

Pat raised his eyebrows. "But I thought you hated the idea of fighting now?"

"I do," she agreed. "But if we invert the churn-pulse circuits in the bazooka and shear the gear run-offs in the squirter we can combine their components to create a primitive outboard motor."

McMoo gasped. "Bo, that's genius! Pure genius!"

"I know!" wailed Bo. "What's wrong with me?"

"We"ll work it out," said Pat kindly. "Now come on, let's go!"

The C.I.A. agents sprinted for the harbour and hopped into the bobbing boat. Pat got busy rowing while Bo and McMoo worked on the weapons.

"How come I can suddenly do stuff like this?" Bo demanded. "Nothing weird happened. I left the *Doodle-Doo*, climbed up a cliff, found this amazing meadow full of juicy grass, had a snack, ran into a barmy bull and a mad cow . . ."

McMoo looked up from his work. "Were they F.B.I. agents?"

"Local cattle, I think. Moobeard had them locked up." Bo shrugged. "Anyway, they attacked me when I tried to help, so I left them to it and roamed the cliffs for hours until I finally saw you . . ."

"Er, guys?" Pat twittered. "Look!" The great wooden door in the cliff had swung open and the silvery ter-moo-nator charged outside onto the dock. Smoke rose from his horns and his beard flapped in the breeze like a demented bat's wing when he spotted the C.I.A. agents.

"A thousand doubloons to the man

who catches them!" Moobeard roared.
"Did Blackbeard ever offer such a
reward? Of course not
– the cheapskate!"
Gaptooth and
Long-Pong dived
into the water and
the other pirates
soon followed, even
the ones with wooden
legs. Pat gulped as they
closed fast on the rowing boat . . .

"There!" cried McMoo, with a final
flourish of crossed wires. "That should
do it!"

"Keep your hooves crossed . . ." Bo
lowered one end of the lash-up into the
water and flicked a switch. "Here goes!"

With a buzz of motors and a faint
whiff of rotten butter, the boat was

suddenly propelled through the water at hair-raising speed. "*Woo-hoooooooo!*" Pat yelled. The gob-smacked pirates faded from sight as the rowing boat zipped away into the band of mist that surrounded the island, and he sighed with relief.

"Where are we going?" Bo wondered.

"To try and find the *Doodle-Doo*," said McMoo. "The Time Shed must still be on board, it's way too big to be unloaded. And if we can't find it we may never get back to our own time!"

The little boat made it through the mist and chugged away for more than an hour. Then Pat saw something close by – a tall wooden pole sticking out of the water.

"A mast," McMoo realized. "Some poor ship sank here."

"And look!" Bo pointed beyond it into the distance. The prow of a ship was protruding from the ocean like a great, wooden beak sniffing the sky. "*Another* sinking ship. That's very odd."

"But *that's* a relief!" Pat pointed due west, to where a ship with a hole in its mainsail bobbed on the horizon. "It must be the *Doodle-Doo!*"

Bo frowned. "But what's that green stuff on the hull?"

She took the boat in closer, and soon all three agents could see precisely what it was. It was grass! Juicy, succulent clumps of grass, sprouting all over the timbers.

"I recognize that grass," said Bo. "It's the same gorgeous, delicious stuff I ate up on the cliff top. The same grass that Moobeard's pirates were digging up in strips and loading on a wheelbarrow . . ."

"It smells delicious." Pat's mouth was watering. "But how can grass grow on wood?"

McMoo looked grave. "I wonder . . ."

Bo switched off the propeller on the

rowing boat, while Pat took hold of a loading rope dangling down from the deck of the *Doodle-Doo*. He tied the end through the rowing boat's rowlocks to secure the little vessel to the bigger ship. Then McMoo started scaling the *Doodle-Doo*'s grassy side, and Pat and

Bo followed him. The gruelling climb seemed to take for ever, but at last they flopped onto the deck — for a strangely soft landing . . .

"Pulsating potatoes!" cried Pat. "The

deck's covered in grass too."

"Oh, dear . . ." The professor swallowed hard. "It seems I was wrong – Moobeard really *does* put pirates like Blackbeard to shame."

Pat frowned. "What do you mean?"

McMoo grabbed hold of Pat and Bo, his eyes wide with alarm. "I think he released those prisoners for one reason only – so they could help him take over the world!"

Chapter Eight

KEEP OFF THE GRASS

"Come on," McMoo commanded, dragging his friends along the length of the quiet ship. "If my theory's right, we'll find proof in the ship's hold . . ."

But before they could get below decks, they ran into Captain Cove and his men, pulling handfuls of grass from the deck. Cove looked up and gasped. "Bless my nautical soul! Are you real, or merely a mirage?"

Pat smiled at Bo. "A *moo*-rage, more like!"

"It's us, all right, Captain Cove!" McMoo shook his hand, and the rest of the crew ran up for a jolly reunion.

"So, your plucky young niece saved you after all, eh?" Cove smiled. "Well done, my dear!"

"Oh! It's you," said Annie-Beth by way of greeting, wobbling out from a nearby cabin. "Didn't expect to see you lot again. How did you catch us up?"

Bo shrugged. "I'm a fast rower."

"Well, this grass is a fast *grower*!" said Cove.

"It's taking over the whole ship,"
Annie-Beth complained. "I've even got
grass growing out of my underclothes!"

"We'll take your word for it," said Pat
quickly.

"The filthy stuff seems to sprout on
absolutely anything," Cove mused. "I
believe it to be a new type of grass
unique to Udderdoom Island."

"I'm afraid it's no natural plant,"
McMoo muttered, glancing at Pat
and Bo. "It's a product of loony F.B.I.
gardening!"

Captain Cove frowned. "Pardon?"

"No time to explain now!" McMoo
dashed off again. "Back in a sec – I've
just got to look in your hold . . ."

McMoo ran down the steep wooden
steps, Bo and Pat just behind him. When
they reached the dimly lit hold, they
got a shock. Aside from the Time Shed,
it seemed empty – save for the clumps
of tall grass growing everywhere, and a

long strip of freshly cut turf lying in the
middle of the space.

"The grass above deck must have
seeded from this," McMoo murmured.
"The pirates cleared out all the cargo
but brought this turf on board."

"It *does* look yummy," Pat agreed, his
tummy rumbling.

"What cow could resist?" said
McMoo, turning to Bo. "I'll bet that the
savage cow and bull you ran into ate
some, just as you did."

"Probably," said Bo. "Like I said, they
were prisoners in a shack on the pasture."

"But they *weren't* prisoners," said McMoo. "They were test cases!" He looked at her. "Did they seem smarter than the average cow as well as nastier?"

"Yes. They caught on really quickly when I explained how to break their chains, and . . . Oh!" Bo gasped. "I understand what you're getting at now, Professor."

Pat frowned. "What?"

Bo turned to him. "After eating some of this mega-grass, a peaceful bull and cow become clever, nasty fighters, right? And a bright, fighting cow like me has turned into a genius who can't bear to fight!"

Pat nodded slowly. "So the grass from Udderdoom Island makes cows more intelligent but reverses their normal nature?"

"Precisely!" she cried. "And that's what Moobeard's up to. First, he attacks twenty ships and brings them back to his lair. Then he hides some mega-grass on board and sends the vessels and their crews on their way again – to France, Spain, England, Holland . . . As the grass spreads through Europe, millions of peaceful cows will eat it – and turn into cruel, savage killers!"

Pat gasped. "Ready and waiting for the F.B.I. to round up and recruit into a cow army that will conquer the world!"

"Oi!" McMoo looked a bit put out. "Doing the explanations is meant to be my job!"

"Sorry, Professor," said Pat. "Well, if this mega-grass spreads so quickly and can grow anywhere, how come Udderdoom Island isn't buried underneath it?"

McMoo smiled. "Remember that niffy mist surrounding the island? It must be some kind of fertilizer spray! When the grass travels through the smoke, it seeds itself super-quickly and grows all over the place."

"Of course!" Bo nodded. "Well, now we know what Moobeard is up to – how are we going to stop him?"

Suddenly, a loud, piercing shriek carried from the deck far above.

"Sounds like Annie-Beth Barmer," Pat realized.

"Professor!" yelled Captain Cove. "Miss Bonnie, Patrick, come quickly!"

"Now what?" Bo raced up the steps behind Pat and McMoo. Annie-Beth was charging about in a wild panic. Cove's crew had to huddle together in case she hit them.

"A pirate ship is coming," Cove cried frantically. "Look! It must be Moobeard again . . . and since his scurvy crew stole our weapons, we cannot fight back at all!"

McMoo stared out to sea. Sure enough, a ship was fast approaching

at full sail. Its body looked like an
enormous upturned insect; the rows
of cannons like stunted legs and the
bowsprit protruding like an evil sting.

A black flag billowed from the tallest mast — and sent a shiver through the professor. "That's not Moobeard's pirate flag," he cried. "It shows a skeleton pointing a spear at a bleeding heart. Sound familiar?"

Pat and Bo swapped baffled glances. But Captain Cove sank to his knees, and his men joined Annie-Beth, racing about in an even wilder panic.

"'Tis the flag of the most dark-hearted, merciless pirate rogue who ever set sail!" groaned Cove. "Forget Moobeard — *mighty Blackbeard himself is attacking this ship!*"

Chapter Nine

BLACKBEARD AHOY!

Pat went rigid with fright. "As if this mega-grass wasn't enough to deal with, now the nastiest pirate of all is going to attack us!"

"I've had better days," McMoo admitted.

Blackbeard's ship, the *Queen Anne's Revenge*, approached with incredible speed. There were dozens of pirates on board, snarling and spitting, waving pistols and swords.

"They'll cut us up and put us in a pie!" Annie-Beth wailed.

"I'm sure Grey Moustache can't be as bad as all that," said Bo.

"*Blackbeard!*" Pat reminded her.

"Whatever. Perhaps he's just misunderstood." Suddenly, a pistol shot echoed out, and Bo's bonnet was blown from her head. "Or maybe not!" she added, quickly ducking.

"We'll have to take all the other passengers to safety in the Time Shed," said McMoo. "There's no other way."

But just as he turned to the others to get their attention, the pirates hurled glass flasks through the air that shattered on the deck and burst into flames. The mega-grass added fuel to the fire, and in a matter of seconds, the way to the cargo hold was blocked.

"We must put out that blaze!" yelled McMoo.

Bo discreetly squirted a thick jet of milk from her udder to try and dampen the fire, while Pat and the professor climbed the rigging and ripped down a sail, hoping to smother it with the billowing fabric.

"Give them a hand," Cove told his men, and they rushed to obey. Even Annie-Beth came wobbling up with a big barrel of drinking water.

"Good thinking!" Pat said approvingly.

"Ta," said Annie-Beth. She drank from the barrel, drained it dry and tossed it over her shoulder. "Well, what are you waiting for? Put out that fire!"

"We've done it!" Bo cheered, coughing on a mouthful of smoke as the last of the flames was extinguished. But the crew had fallen strangely silent.

"Too late," breathed Captain Cove.

"The *Doodle-Doo*'s been boarded!"

The smoke blew away and a gang of vicious-looking pirates was revealed, standing on the deck behind a massive, fearsome figure. His glowering face was as grimy and rumpled as his long crimson coat. Matted black hair coiled down about his shoulders. Two blood-stained cutlasses were tucked into his belt, and the leather straps across his chest held six powerful pistols. But it was the big black face-fuzz that held Pat transfixed. It was so wild and enormous it made Moobeard's beard look like a goatee! Cannon fuses had been carefully tied into it and set alight to finish the effect of brute, powerful menace.

"Hello!" said Bo cheerfully, holding

out a hoof in welcome. "You must be Turquoise Nosehair – um, *Blackbeard* – and friends! Won't you please sit down?"

"Wench, stop yer prattling!" thundered Blackbeard, while most of Cove's crew gibbered with fear. "Now listen, ye yellow-bellied sap-suckers! My boys and me have attacked *nineteen* ships in these parts this morning, and we've found not a sniff of loot – only grass! So, I sank the lot of them."

"Nineteen ships in one morning? No wonder you're a pirate legend." McMoo glared at him. "We passed two of them on our way here. What did you do with the people on board?"

"I had no choice," the pirate king growled. "I'd got nothing of value so I marooned them on a deserted island nearby – they should fetch me a fair ransom at least."

"Phew!" McMoo cried. "Those people are all safe for now, and Moobeard's grass that was on board those ships is lying at the bottom of the ocean where it can do no more harm."

"Silence!" The imposing pirate gazed coldly at McMoo. "I warn ye, my mood's as black as my beard today – so tell me, what treasures do ye have aboard?"

Captain Cove stepped forward nervously. "Er . . . we have nothing. We have been looted already by that devil Moobeard."

"Moobeard?" Blackbeard grabbed Cove by the shoulders. "Why, the

boneless upstart!"

"No fighting, please!" squeaked Bo.

"That metal-faced milksop is trying to steal my reputation as greatest of all pirates!" bellowed Blackbeard. "How dare he rob you afore I ... I ..." He shoved Cove aside when he caught sight of Annie-Beth. "Ahoy! So that vile pretender has not taken all yer riches, I see? Here is a jewel more precious than any I've spied in many a long year, eh, lads?"

"What?" Pat nodded towards Annie-Beth. "You mean ... that?"

"Why, sir!" Annie-Beth blushed and had to fan herself with her bonnet. "Your words are like honey, and you are most pleasing to my widow's eye. My name is Annie-Beth," She gave him a coy smile. "I have feared your pirate's reputation for so long — but if you would truly treasure me, sir, I'd never fear anything again!"

"Apart from his smoking beard setting her dress on fire," Bo murmured.

"It do be love at first sight!" Blackbeard proclaimed, and Annie-Beth squealed as he grabbed her in a bear-hug.

"Awww," said Blackbeard's pirates, and gave their captain a round of applause.

"I don't believe it!" cried McMoo. "Blackbeard and Annie-Beth have turned a pirate hijacking into a love story!"

"I *knew* he must be misunderstood!" Bo sniffed. "Isn't it beautiful?"

Pat grimaced. "No!"

"Er, Mrs Barmer," Captain Cove began. "The newspapers say that Blackbeard has thirteen wives already!"

"Who's counting?" Annie-Beth pulled playfully on Blackbeard's smoking beard. "But you must prove your love for me, sir!"

"Name the deed and I'll do it, my sweet apple," cried the pirate, "however wicked!"

"You must sail to Udderdoom Island and get back all my beautiful belongings," Annie-Beth told him. "In fact, there's loads of loot there – nineteen ships' worth, so I'm told. And I'd like it all, please!"

McMoo frowned. "That's outrageous!"

"True," Annie-Beth agreed.

"Ha! I likes yer style, Annie!"

Blackbeard turned to his crew. "What say you, lads — shall we storm Moobeard's island and steal his riches?"

The pirates gave a resounding cheer and jumped about in excitement — even a pirate with two wooden legs who quickly fell over. As Captain Cove and his crew stared on in baffled relief, the C.I.A. agents quickly conferred.

"I didn't see this coming," Pat admitted.

"Me neither," said Bo. "And while one lot of pirates fights the other, we must find a way to destroy the mega-grass that's left. But how?"

"To create it and brew up the fertilizer, Moobeard must have some kind of high-tech lab on the island," McMoo reasoned. "If we can find it, perhaps I can create some weedkiller or something."

"Great plan," said Pat. "All we need to do now is stay alive long enough to put it into practice . . ."

"Enough jumping up and down, me hearties!" hollered Blackbeard, raising his bloody cutlass in the air. "Cap'n Cove, will ye and all those aboard agree to fight for me, or must I throw you overboard here and now?"

Cove gulped. McMoo nudged him. "Very well," the captain said. "We will do as you ask."

"Then let us set sail for Udderdoom Island," shouted Blackbeard. "*HA-HARRRRRR!*"

Chapter Ten

PIRATE-ITUDE PROBLEMS

Pat, Bo and McMoo stood with Captain Cove, watching Blackbeard and Annie-Beth at the ship's wheel. The pirate had taken control of the *Doodle-Doo* while his first mate, Isaac, helmed the *Queen Anne's Revenge*. Both ships were on a course for Udderdoom Island.

Pat could see thick patches of grass growing already on the side of Blackbeard's boat; a grim reminder of the real battle that laid ahead – a struggle not only for the future of all cowkind, but to save history itself from plunging into chaos.

"Land in sight!" Blackbeard hollered

suddenly, making everyone jump.
Pat looked ahead. A sea-cold shiver
ran through him when he saw the
misty crags and staring stone face of
Udderdoom Island rising up from the
water.

Blackbeard's pirates got busy in the
rigging, working the sails to speed
the *Doodle-Doo* on her way. The
Queen Anne's Revenge quickened too,
her cannons at the ready as the fog-
shrouded isle grew closer . . .

Then, suddenly, a large ship
loomed silently out of the mist
ahead. Pat gasped – it was the *Beefy
Bandit,* Moobeard's vessel! There was
no sign of the villainous ter-moo-nator
himself, but Gaptooth and Long-Pong
stood at the helm, backed by their pirate
gang.

"Turn ye back, dogs of the sea!"
Gaptooth yelled. "Or feel the wrath of
Moobeard."

"Heave to!" Blackbeard stamped
forward to the *Doodle-Doo*'s bowsprit and
waved his fist, as his crew rushed to bring
the ship to a stop. "Ye dare to threaten *I*,
wretch? Know ye not who I am?"

A loud, collective gasp went up from
the pirates aboard the *Beefy Bandit*.

"It's Auntie Muriel!" cried Big Pete in
delight.

Gaptooth cuffed the pirate round
the head. "You half-blind fool! That be
Blackbeard!"

"Oh." Big Pete looked disappointed.

"Now, where be Moobeard, ye mud-wallowing milksops?" Blackbeard demanded.

"He toils in his island fortress," called Long-Pong. "He was not expecting enemies to call till tomorrow at the earliest!"

"A *real* pirate expects enemies at any time!" roared Blackbeard. "Now, the *Queen Anne's Revenge* is packed with cannons and I've armed this ship to the gills too! Surrender at once – or else!"

Pat chewed his lip. "What a bluff."

McMoo nodded. "Let's hope that mob believe him!"

"If we *do* surrender," called Gaptooth cautiously. "Will ye let us live?"

"Certainly not!" boomed Blackbeard. "I'll make ye walk the plank into a shark's open mouth and send the bits of yer bodies home to yer mothers!"

The crew of the *Beefy Bandit* reflected on this. "Quite right," several said. "Spoken like a true pirate," others agreed.

Annie-Beth looked shocked. "You can't kill them like that, Blackie — the sight of sharks makes my knees go funny!"

Blackbeard considered this, then waved his cutlass. "I'll tell ye what, me hearties. Why not turn on your measly master, Moobeard, and fight *for* me instead of against me?"

"Great idea!" said McMoo, doing a little stirring. "You could work for a *proper* pirate for a change!"

"Us, turn against Moobeard?" Long-Pong's bottom made a nervous interruption. "But that be . . . mutiny!"

"'Tis true." Big Pete nodded. "There can be no greater crime at sea."

Blackbeard covered his nose. "Aside

from that man's bum letting off, that is!"

The pirates considered for a moment.

"Ye know, lads," said Gaptooth, "it was criminal the way Moobeard let them European sea-knaves sail off as free men instead of holding them for a ransom."

"I caught 'em again, me hearties," growled Blackbeard. "I marooned them, and I'll ransom each and every one."

"Hooray!" shouted the pirates, who enjoyed a bit of marooning.

"And ye know something else?" said Long-Pong. "There have been times when I've secretly thought that Moobeard's beard is . . . a falsie!"

Gasps of horror went up from the pirate crew.

"A pirate without a true beard?" wailed one.

"'Tis unthinkable!" another agreed.

Gaptooth looked at each pirate in turn. And then he grinned: "That's the clincher, Cap'n Blackbeard — we'll serve ye instead!"

McMoo, Bo and Pat hugged each other as a great cheer went up, not only from the relieved crew of the *Doodle-Doo*, but from the *Queen Anne's Revenge* and the *Beefy Bandit* too.

"Turn then, me hearties!" Blackbeard shouted. "And let's bring hellfire and ruination to that old silver bull, Moobeard!"

With three ships now under his command, Blackbeard set off again in boisterous spirits.

Captain Cove cheered. "I'm so glad there won't be any fighting."

"Me too!" said Bo excitedly.

Pat grinned at the professor. "Now,

if we can just get rid of Moobeard's mega-grass and persuade him to push off back to the future, it's case closed!"

"Don't let's get cocky," said McMoo. "That ter-moo-nator might be outnumbered, but he's extra tricky. And I've got a feeling he'll have something up his sleeve . . ."

As the ships pierced through the choking veil of fertilizer mist and entered the harbour, Blackbeard rubbed his hands. "Udderdoom Island and all its lovely loot," he roared. "Soon it will all be mine!"

But suddenly, a huge, deep rumbling noise started up, and the quiet harbour waters began to churn around them as though a billion sharks were feasting beneath the surface. Annie-Beth squealed and clutched hold of Blackbeard. "What's happening?"

"Oh, no!" cried Gaptooth from the *Beefy Bandit*. "He's started the engines!"

"You and Moobeard talked about engines on the beach," Pat recalled. "*What* engines?"

"My job was to make sure they were fully loaded," said Gaptooth, quailing. "But I didn't think he could work them by himself . . ."

"All along, Moobeard was plotting to leave us behind!" Long-Pong scowled. "Cheek!"

The rumbling was getting worse, and now massive waves were buffeting the ships. "I don't understand!" yelled Captain Cove over the din. "It's as if we were drifting further and further away from the island . . ."

"You've got it the wrong way round," McMoo told him, wide-eyed. "We're not drifting away from the island – *it's* drifting away from *us*!"

116

Bo gasped. "Engines strong enough to push a whole island through the water?"

"It must be a giant sea ship from the future which the F.B.I. has *disguised* as an island," McMoo realized, "with massive propellers installed beneath the surface."

"No wonder he wasn't worried about all those prisoners sending the navy back here." Pat flinched as a huge wave crashed over the side of the *Doodle-Doo*. "He knew he'd be long gone."

"We'll disappear ourselves, if this keeps up!" roared Blackbeard as the ship pitched this way and that on the whipped-up waters. "Our ships will sink to the bottom of the sea – aye, and our bones with them!"

"Moobeard is truly a devil if he can bend nature to his will in this way!" Cove was as white as a sheet, clinging on to the nearest mast. "We're doomed . . . All of us *doomed*!"

Chapter Eleven

UTTER DOOM ON UDDERDOOM

"Oh, stop moaning, the lot of you!" Annie-Beth wailed as the misty, self-propelled island chugged further and further away. "Somebody do something – my lovely loot is escaping!"

Pat shook off a seasick feeling. "Professor, what *can* we do? Even if the *Doodle-Doo* stays afloat, we'll never catch up with Moobeard!"

McMoo staggered over the lurching deck to the port side of the stricken ship. "There's just one chance . . ."

"The rowing boat!" Bo cried. "Of course, our home-made outboard motor is still inside."

118

"Hang in there, Blackbeard, and follow us if you can!" the professor shouted. "We must stop Moobeard – even if it's the last thing we do."

A massive wave sploshed over Pat's face. "It'll probably be the wettest!"

"Wait!" roared Blackbeard, tossing McMoo a sword. "Take one o' my cutlasses."

McMoo caught it and beamed. "Thanks!"

"Why did you take that?" Bo asked. "You would never use it."

"True – but what a souvenir! Blackbeard's cutlass, imagine that . . ." McMoo grinned, and shoved it through his belt. "From cutlass to *cow*-tlass. Come on!"

Soaked by sea spray and clinging on for their lives, the C.I.A. agents climbed down the slippery ropes and into the little rowing boat. It was half filled with water, and Pat and McMoo desperately bailed it out while Bo fiddled with the motor. After a few seconds the engine spluttered into life, and the boat leaped away, riding the choppy waves left in the wake of Moobeard's disappearing island.

"Luckily that F.B.I. base is too big to move very fast," said McMoo.

"But it's got a headstart on us." Pat coughed. "And that misty smokescreen is choking me!"

"Relax, boys. We'll soon break through and catch up with Moobeard – easy as A-B-*Sea*!" So saying, Bo hung over the edge of the boat, dipped her lower body in the turbulent Caribbean waters and released a huge burst of milk from her udder! Propelled now by milk-jets as well as an outboard motor, the rowing boat started to gain on Moobeard's travelling lair. In a matter of minutes, the C.I.A. agents had passed through the eerie mist and were pulling up alongside the wooden jetty.

"Keep squirting, Bo!" McMoo urged her. "Pat, get ready to jump for dry land!"

Leaping with all his strength, Pat hurtled through the air and landed safely on his belly. He reached out a hoof to help up the professor, then the two of them reached out to Bo and pulled her onto dry land.

"We did it!" Pat cheered.

But there was no time for congratulating each other. The big wooden door to Moobeard's base opened up in the cliff side and there, framed against the darkness beyond, stood the same belligerent grey bull and mad milk cow

Bo had tangled with earlier.

"Uh-oh," said Pat, as Moobeard's test cases began to growl and drool. "Looks like we've got a fight on our hooves!"

McMoo stood protectively in front of Bo as the battle-hungry cattle charged forwards. But to Pat's surprise, Bo somersaulted over the professor's head and met her two attackers with a flurry of punches and kung-*moo* chops. The bull gasped as she conked him on the head with a double-hoofed haymaker, and the milk cow mooed in surprise as Bo got her in an udder lock and hurled her to the ground.

A grin spread over Pat's face. "Little Bo – you just had a fight!"

"Tell me," asked the professor urgently, "what's the square root of seven hundred-and-one?"

Bo shrugged. "Who cares?"

"That's my big sis!" Pat ran over and hugged her tight. "Bo, you're back to normal!"

"You'd better believe it!" Bo cried, holding both hands up in the air like she'd just won a boxing match. "And Moobeard had better believe it too!"

"It seems the effects of the mega-grass must wear off when its victims stop eating the stuff," McMoo deduced. "Which is good news for the test cases – they should get better once they're back eating normal grass."

"Great." Bo flexed her hooves. "But right now we've got other fish to fry." She glanced down at the water and noticed a bream swimming close to the jetty. "Um, no offence."

"Let's go," said McMoo, leading the way into the ter-moo-nator's evil lair.

The tunnels were long and gloomy and the rock walls throbbed with the power of the island's deep-sea engines.

"I can smell chemicals," Pat whispered.

They ran on, following the stink, down through the winding tunnels until they came to a large, steel door marked KEEP OUT – MOOBEARD'S PRIVATE LAIR.

"Oh, well, we'd better not go in then," said Bo, smirking. "I *don't* think!" She whirled round on one rear hoof and kicked out with the other. The steel door buckled under the blow. Then, combining their strength, Pat and the professor lowered their heads and charged at the door, smashing it off its hinges. Their momentum carried them into the brightly lit room beyond, and Bo leaped in after them . . .

She gave a low, impressed whistle.

Not only was this an underground laboratory, it was plainly also the nerve centre of Udderdoom Island. Facing away from them was a huge, high-backed pilot's seat; it sat in front of the bank of levers, switches and steering wheels that lined the far wall. A mass of monitors overhead showed the island from many different angles. The biggest screen showed green, wide-open sea, which was presumably the view ahead.

To the left and right of the room, several long lab benches were cluttered with scientific gizmos, colourful test tubes and clumps of mega-grass in buckets. An enormous pile of the stuff had been heaped at the back of the room, perhaps for further testing.

"Typical ter-moo-nator," McMoo muttered. "No kettle, no tea bags, nothing!"

Together the C.I.A. agents advanced on the big chair.

"Give it up, Moobeard," said the professor. "We've spoiled your plans, your men have turned against you and there's nowhere to run — not from us *or* Blackbeard."

"Yeah, come on, Beardie, it's no good sulking . . ." Impulsively, Bo grabbed the back of the chair and spun it round — but as she did so, it pulled on a hidden trip wire! A butter-bazooka concealed on one of the benches spat into vicious life, and the three agents

were instantly drenched in yellow, slippery goo.

"Not again!" Pat gasped. He slipped helplessly and banged his head. Bo grabbed hold of the chair for support, but it upended and crashed down on top of her. McMoo tried to help his friends, but the jet of scalding-hot butter was too intense to withstand. He fell too, with a smelly splash – just as a massive, powerful figure emerged from its hiding place in the heap of mega-grass at the back of the room.

"My savage cattle delayed you long enough for me to set my trap," grated

127

Moobeard, his green eye aglow, his large beard bristling. "You have come here to your doom, C.I.A. scum. And there is no escape."

The ter-moo-nator stalked menacingly towards them . . .

Chapter Twelve

SCUTTLED AT LAST!

McMoo heard Pat and Bo groan in a buttery daze, too out of it to help him now.

"Listen, Moobeard," he began, using the trip wire to pull himself up. "Just because we've trashed your mission, left you a laughing stock and ruined years of planning, is that any reason to kill us? Why not shave that silly beard, take off your eye patch and make a *moo* start?"

"The setback is minimal," Moobeard snarled as he stamped closer, pulling out a ray gun. "My mission will continue."

The professor frowned. "But most of the mega-grass you sneaked onto those boats is now lying at the bottom of the sea."

"So?" The ter-moo-nator pointed to the huge pile behind him. "I have an endless supply of treated grass on this island, and I am constantly improving it – to make it spread faster, to make it almost unbearably tasty and completely addictive, so cows and bulls will eat it in ever-greater volumes. It starts altering their minds in milliseconds . . ."

McMoo backed away as the pirate creature continued his advance. "Where are you taking this island?"

"I will settle off the south coast of Africa and attack ships there." The ter-moo-nator grinned through his scary beard, aiming his gun straight at McMoo. "Then I shall pillage the Indian trading routes, spreading my grass right across Asia!"

"Nice idea," said McMoo nervously. "Just make sure no one throws a spanner

in the works." He suddenly grinned. "Or
a *cutlass*!"

With that, he spun round and hurled
Blackbeard's sword at the island's control
systems! It struck an instrument panel
with a shower of sparks.

"*NOOOOOO!*" roared Moobeard.
He fired the ray gun . . .

But as he did so, Bo and Pat grabbed
the professor's hooves and pulled them
from under him. As he fell to the floor,
the death ray whizzed past his snout
and into the heart of the controls!

This time the damage was far more impressive. Alarms blared. Red lights flashed. The whole island lurched as its powerful engines misfired, spluttered and then went into reverse!

McMoo beamed at his buttery friends. "Good work, you two!"

"Are you sure?" Pat fretted. "The whole island's going backwards!"

"And so is Moobeard!" Bo yelled, kicking the pilot's chair across the slippery floor. It crashed into the ter-moo-nator and sent him staggering into the big pile of mega-grass. His roars of rage turned to mechanical splutters as the greenery got into his mouth. He swallowed down one mouthful, then another. The C.I.A. agents watched in amazement as the ter-moo-nator tucked in to the succulent leaves like a ravenous animal, gobbling up more and more!

"Looks like Moobeard made this latest batch of mega-grass just a little *too* tasty," said the professor happily. "Not even *he* can resist it!"

"But ter-moo-nators love fighting, even more than I do," Bo realized. "And if that stuff does to him what it did to me . . ."

Moobeard raised himself from the debris. He slowly turned to face McMoo, Pat and Bo.

And then he held out his arms!

"How about a group hug?" Moobeard warbled.

Pat blinked. "Pardon?"

"I am very sorry," the ter-moo-nator

went on. "I have been a very naughty quasi-robotic bull. How can I make amends?"

McMoo frowned. "Could you show us how to get rid that treated grass for good?"

"Of course." Moobeard trotted obediently over to a lab bench and produced three large stoppered test tubes. "A few drops of twenty-sixth-century weed-killer will destroy it without harming the environment."

Pat eagerly snatched the test tubes and shoved them down his shirt. "Wa-*hay*!"

"And look!" Bo pointed to a flickering monitor screen. It showed three familiar sailing ships fast approaching. "Blackbeard and the others have caught us up."

The island suddenly juddered alarmingly and tilted to one side. "Not a moment too soon!" McMoo declared. "I think Moobeard's managed to scuttle his own island. The controls are burning out. We've stopped going backwards – but now we're starting to sink!"

"The bottom of the sea is the best place for Udderdoom Island," said Moobeard meekly. "Let it remain a sunken monument to a bull's mad folly."

"Awww, doesn't he talk nice?" Bo shoved the ter-moo-nator towards the door. "Now shift your silver bum, beard-face – we've got to get out of here!"

The cattle were back outside within minutes, but already the dock was dipping beneath the waves. With extraordinary strength and unlikely gentleness, Moobeard lifted the grey bull and the cow into the rowing boat. "You will soon return to normal after feeding on ordinary grass again."

"And I'm sorry for any bruises!" Bo added, jumping in beside the three of them.

The cow and the bull looked at each other blankly, and lay back down in a daze. McMoo and Pat squeezed into the rowing boat beside them as the *Doodle-Doo* pulled up alongside.

"Avast there!" came Blackbeard's

throaty holler. "So ye caught that black-hearted rogue, eh?"

The ter-moo-nator lowered his head, humbly. "I am very sorry for copying your beard and pretending to be a pirate."

Blackbeard pulled out two of his pistols. "Ye *will* be!"

"Arrrrrr!" Gaptooth agreed from the deck of the *Beefy Bandit*, as his crew jeered and pointed their butter-bazookas and sour-cream squirters.

Moobeard faced them all. "I would also like to apologize for treating my crew so meanly, and for—"

"All right, Beardy, this isn't speech time at the Pirate Oscars!" said Bo impatiently, catching hold of the long rope dangling from the *Doodle-Doo*. "Prof, I think I liked him better when I could whack him!"

"Blackbeard, Gaptooth and the others will do more than that if they get their hands on him," said McMoo grimly. He pulled out a large silver plate from behind the ter-moo-nator's armoured back — an F.B.I. time-travel machine — and got busy reprogramming the controls. "I'm going to send him straight to Director Yak in the twenty-sixth century . . ."

"Thank you," droned Moobeard, as the professor placed the silver plate under the ter-moo-nator's chunky feet. Black smoke began to envelop the robo-bull. "I look forward to being locked up so that I can learn the error of my ways . . ."

He faded away to nothing.

Captain Cove stared. Blackbeard gulped. And yet another gasp of horror went up from the pirates of the *Beefy Bandit*.

"Witchcraft!" wailed Long-Pong.

"Now, throw Moobeard's wicked weapons overboard, you sea-dogs," McMoo commanded. "Before *you* disappear too!"

"Aye, do it, brothers!" cried Gaptooth. He and his fellow pirates hastily hurled their futuristic guns to the bottom of the briny sea. "And then let's be away from here, lest we be cursed as well!"

"I'm with ye there, my fine lads!" Blackbeard shouted. He grabbed

Annie-Beth's hand and ran to the other side of the *Doodle-Doo*, where the slightly grassy *Queen Anne's Revenge* was pulling alongside. "We'll weigh anchor and take our leave of these law-abiding sailors . . . !"

"But what about my belongings and the rest of the loot!" cried Annie-Beth as Udderdoom Island slowly disappeared beneath the waves. "You're letting it all sink! Call yourself a pirate?"

"She doesn't need pirates now," Pat laughed, "she needs scuba-divers!"

"I"m sorry, my sweet banana," said Blackbeard, scrambling across the boarding nets to the *Queen Anne's Revenge*. "But there still be a ransom to be had on those men I marooned on Sacramost Isle . . ."

"Forget that bunch, they're not worth the bother!" The nets sagged dangerously as Annie-Beth crawled over to join him. "What you need to do is

140

rob loads of Spanish galleons and give me all their rubies and gold . . ."

"Whatever ye say, my little coconut," Blackbeard agreed quickly. "The hostages may go free. Now, let us speed from here, afore any more of Moobeard's wizardry can do us harm!"

"Wait!" Pat shouted. He pulled a test tube from his shirt and hurled it up at the pirate. "Pour this stuff on any weird grass you find and you'll get rid of it in no time!"

Blackbeard caught it in one big hand. "Much obliged to ye. Fare ye well!"

Leaving the bull and the cow asleep in the rowing boat, McMoo, Bo and Pat climbed back up the rope and crawled onto the *Doodle-Doo*'s deck.

"I-I don't believe it!" said Captain Cove, as the *Queen Anne's Revenge* started to turn, the wind filling its sails. "Blackbeard's leaving us unharmed – and he's taking that wretched Annie-Beth Barmer with him!" He danced for joy, and the sailors sang merrily in the rigging. "We're free of them both!"

"And you'll soon be free of this silly grass too," said Bo, as Pat splashed the greenery with drops from another test tube. The grass withered to dust in seconds.

"Now, Captain Cove," said McMoo briskly. "A couple of things – do you know where Sacramost Isle is?"

He nodded. "It's nearby, on the way to Jamaica."

"Then perhaps you could pick up those people Blackbeard marooned and give them a lift." He smiled. "Oh, and please take the cattle in the rowing boat to Jamaica with you, and set them free."

"Very well," Cove agreed, scratching his head. "But where are *you* going?"

"Patrick and Bonnie and I have got to see a man about a shed." McMoo grinned. "Bye-bye!"

With that, the C.I.A. agents dashed away below decks. A few more splashes from Pat and the hold was a mega-grass-free zone.

"Will Blackbeard and Annie-Beth be happy together, Professor?" asked Pat, as they entered their ramshackle shed.

"Not for long, I'm afraid," said McMoo. "Old Blackbeard comes to a

very nasty end before the year is out.
The law catches up with him and he
loses his head . . ." He gazed into the
distance for a few seconds. "Still! 'A
short life and a merry one' – that's the
pirate motto."

"Annie-Beth will be all right, of
course," Bo grumbled.

Pat nodded. "She'll probably retire
with her late-husband's riches and spend
her days moaning to her neighbours,
boring them all to death!"

Suddenly, the image of a burly black
bull appeared on the main computer
screen.

"Hey, it's Yakky-baby!" Bo cried
fondly. "How's tricks?"

"Good, thanks to you!" Director Yak
nodded. "We've got that weird ter-moo-
nator you sent – but what have you
done to him? He insisted we lock him
up at once before he could do any more
damage. Then he asked for a guitar so

he could play us all gentle folk songs!"

"His change of attitude will wear off soon, I'm afraid," said McMoo ruefully. "But at least the F.B.I.'s little Caribbean holiday is over for good."

"And I reckon we've earned *ourselves* a holiday," Pat declared.

"We've got one!" said Bo, punching the air. "Bessie Barmer is away from the farm for two whole weeks, remember? On her own Caribbean break."

"Really?" Yak pressed some buttons on a laptop beside him and smirked. "Well, checking the weather records for the local time zone, it looks like Bessie has chosen the worst possible moment to go. Over the next fortnight she'll have rain, fog − and the only Caribbean hailstones in recorded history!"

"Oh, dear, what a shame!" said McMoo. "Let's have a big cup of tea and celebrate!"

"Enjoy your time without her," said Yak. "But you can be sure I'll have another mission for you soon."

Pat pulled out the kettle. "I hope so!"

"Bring it on!" Bo agreed, plopping tea bags in the teapot. "Even if it means tangling with pirates again."

"Perhaps some day we will." McMoo smiled. "But one thing's for sure, pirates or no pirates − as C.I.A. agents, we always end up with an adventure to *treasure*!"

THE END

The Cows in Action will return soon
in **THE MOO-GIC OF MERLIN**

COW-ER WITH FEAR!

Genius cow Professor McMoo and his trusty sidekicks, Pat and Bo, are star agents of the C.I.A. – short for COWS IN ACTION! They travel through time, fighting evil bulls from the future and keeping history on the right track . . .

In ANCIENT EGYPT, a monstrous *moo-my* has come to life and kicked the PHARAOH off his throne. Sent to investigate, the C.I.A. agents face PERIL in the pyramids and nightmares on the Nile. Can they foil a TERRIFYING time-crime before the whole WORLD falls to the moo-my's curse?

It's time for action.